Dear Parent:

The moral of this charming story should be, "Sometimes it takes a village, working together long into the night, to help a friend in distress."

Clifford's situation will be familiar to most young children because they, too, may have spent a wonderful day away— maybe at Grandma's house; or with a friend on a great outing to a ballgame, the zoo, or the planetarium; or just hanging out. In the daylight there is the thrill of adventure and a taste of freedom, along with your favorite picnic food. But when night falls and the covers of a strange bed are turned down, the sudden longing for home and family is overwhelming.

It's difficult to predict which children will feel the strongest pangs of loneliness. Sometimes a shy one may be fine, while a daytime boaster or a big guy like Clifford could fall apart. So it's a good idea for adults to be prepared. The first few sleep overs are wisely spent an easy distance from home, should the urgent need for rescue arise. In this story, Clifford doesn't have that option, so it's a long, hard night for all concerned. Fortunately for him, he and Emily Elizabeth have many loyal friends who work together to provide comfort in his time of great need. Their caring, cooperative efforts ease his pain and eventually, surrounded by friends, he is able to sleep.

This story not only offers an opportunity to listen to what kids have to say about separation, but also underscores the value of working together as a team for a very good cause.

Adele M. Brodkin, Ph.D.

Visit Clifford at scholastic.com/clifford

ISBN 0-439-22364-4

Library of Congress Cataloging-in-Publication Data is available

10 9 8 7 6 5 4 3 2 1   01 02 03 04 05 06

Printed in the U.S.A.   24
First printing, March 2001

Clifford THE BIG RED DOG®

The Big Sleep Over

Adapted by David L. Harrison

Illustrated by Ken Edwards

**Based on the Scholastic book series
"Clifford The Big Red Dog"
by Norman Bridwell**

From the television script
"Clifford's Big Sleep Over" by Larry Swerdlove

Cartwheel ·B·O·O·K·S·®

SCHOLASTIC INC.

New York   Toronto   London   Auckland   Sydney   Mexico City
New Delhi   Hong Kong

"Emily Elizabeth! No more fretting!
No more sighing! No more petting!
You'll make us miss your cousin's wedding!
Say good-bye to Clifford, please!"

"Good-bye, Clifford. You be good.

Do what Charley says you should.

We'd take you with us if we could,

But puppies make my cousin sneeze."

"Come on, Clifford! Just for fun,
Let's see how fast that we can run!
Clifford, I give up! You won!
Aren't you glad that we can play?

"Come on, boy! Let's play some ball!
Wow! You make the ball look small!
Wow! You knocked it over the wall!
Aren't we having fun today?"

"Clifford's played and he's been fed.

He's yawning like a sleepyhead.

Come on, Clifford, time for bed.

You'll soon be sleeping like a log.

Poor, poor Clifford feels so bad.
The best, best friend he's ever had
Has gone away and left him sad."

"T-Bone? T-Bone? What's that sound?
Sounds like Emily's big red hound!
Sounds like the saddest dog around!"

"A big red dog should not be blue.

There must be something we can do.

Let's go see how we can help!"

"Excuse me, people. Coming through.
We've got to figure what to do
So he can sleep—and we can, too!"

"Everybody sleeps with toys,
From puppy dogs to girls and boys.
These will help you stop that noise!"

Yowwwwwww

"When my daughter couldn't sleep, I'd
Take her for a nice long ride,
And she'd start snoring by my side.
Does anybody have a truck?

"No more yelping. No more growling.
Clifford finally stopped his yowling!
He's too sleepy now for howling.
Soon he'll fall asleep, with luck."

"Someone think of some new trick!

Make it clever!

Make it slick!

Make it work!

And make it quick—

Before we fall in one big heap!"

"Lonesome Clifford, in your tent,
Wondering where your Emily went,
We're your friends that Emily sent
So you can close your eyes and sleep."

"Go on, Clifford, close your eyes.
We'll sleep beneath the starry skies
And wake up to a big surprise!
Shhh. Don't make another peep.

Mustn't worry. Mustn't fret.

Clifford, you're a faithful pet.

Your dear Emily will be home yet.

In the morning you will see.

"You made it, Clifford, through the night!
That sun sure is a welcome sight!
Now who would make this day just right?
Who's that coming? Could it be?"

"Clifford! Clifford! What a joy!

I'm so lucky to have you, boy!

Look! I brought you a nice stuffed toy!

How did you do while I was gone?

"Clifford, I don't understand
Why all our friends are on the sand!
I wonder why they're all on hand.
Clifford, what's been going on?"

"He would tell you, yes, he would.
He would tell you if he could.
So I will tell you what he should.
Clifford, in his way, was good."

BOOKS IN THIS SERIES:

Welcome to Birdwell Island: Everyone on Birdwell Island thinks that Clifford is just too big! But when there's an emergency, Clifford The Big Red Dog teaches everyone to have respect—even for those who are different.

A Puppy to Love: Emily Elizabeth's birthday wish comes true: She gets a puppy to love! And with her love and kindness, Clifford The Small Red Puppy becomes Clifford The Big Red Dog!

The Big Sleep Over: Clifford has to spend his first night without Emily Elizabeth. When he has trouble falling asleep, his Birdwell Island friends work together to make sure that he—and everyone else—gets a good night's sleep.

No Dogs Allowed: No dogs in Birdwell Island Park? That's what Mr. Bleakman says—before he realizes that sharing the park with dogs is much more fun.

An Itchy Day: Clifford has an itchy patch! He's afraid to go to the vet, so he tries to hide his scratching from Emily Elizabeth. But Clifford soon realizes that it's better to be truthful and trust the person he loves most—Emily Elizabeth.

The Doggy Detectives: Oh, no! Emily Elizabeth is accused of stealing Jetta's gold medal—and then her shiny mirror! But her dear Clifford never doubts her innocence and, with his fellow doggy detectives, finds the real thief.

Follow the Leader: While playing follow the leader with Clifford and T-Bone, Cleo learns that playing fair is the best way to play!

The Big Red Mess: Clifford tries to stay clean for the Dog of the Year contest, but he ends up becoming a big red mess! However, when Clifford helps the judge reach the shore safely, he finds that he doesn't need to stay clean to be the Dog of the Year.

The Big Surprise: Poor Clifford. It's his birthday, but none of his friends will play with him. Maybe it's because they're all busy... planning his surprise party!

The Wild Ice Cream Machine: Charley and Emily Elizabeth decide to work the ice cream machine themselves. Things go smoothly... until the lever gets stuck and they find themselves knee-deep in ice cream!

Dogs and Cats: Can dogs and cats be friends? Clifford, T-Bone, and Cleo don't think so. But they have a change of heart after they help two lost kittens find their mother.

The Magic Ball: Emily Elizabeth trusts Clifford to deliver a package to the post office, but he opens it and breaks the gift inside. Clifford tries to hide his blunder, but Emily Elizabeth appreciates honesty and understands that accidents happen.